Lockdown Rhymes

About the author

Kev Reynolds is a travel writer with more than fifty books to his name. Most of these are published by Cicerone Press (www.cicerone.co.uk) and devoted to mountain and countryside regions as far apart as Southern England and the high Himalaya. He has also published two volumes of memoirs: A Walk in the Clouds and Abode of the Gods. The first of these is a collection of 75 short stories gathered from fifty years of mountain adventure; the second describes eight of his trekking expeditions in Nepal. This is his second book of verse, a companion volume to Rambling Rhymes – many of the subjects of these rhymes are based on people he's met and places explored during his travels. He lives in rural contentment in the Kentish countryside. (www.kevreynolds.co.uk)

Lockdown Rhymes

by Kev Reynolds

illustrated by Clare Crooke

© Kev Reynolds (words) 2020
© Clare Crooke (illustrations) 2020
ISBN: 9798681654254

All rights reserved. No part of this publication may be reproduced or transmitted in any form or by any means without prior written permission of the copyright holder.

Privately published by the author at www.kevreynolds.co.uk

Acknowledgements

My thanks to Françoise Besson and Ian Maple for their insistence that I should publish these poems in a book, and to Clare Crooke and Siân Pritchard-Jones for making it possible. And, of course, special thanks to my wife for getting us both through Lockdown with love and laughter

Dedicated to
Min, Paul, Charlie and Will

Contents

Introduction

I've always imagined poets as earnest-looking men and women who lead tragic lives and die young. So let me say straight away, I'm not a poet. My face remains more or less free from worry lines, I've led anything but a tragic life, and now that I'm ancient I've dodged any chance of dying young.

No, I'm not a poet. So please don't judge the nonsense you read here as if they are poems.

Poems can be real works of art. And like many forms of art, if they're to be truly appreciated, an emotional response from the reader is called for. While I can honestly say that on the whole I enjoy poetry and have a number of volumes on my bookshelves, some poets bury their message so deeply that even after many readings I'm still baffled as to what they're about.

But give me the light-hearted rhymes of Robert Service, Edward Lear or Pam Ayres, and I'm away. I brought my children up on The Cremation of Sam McGee, and on several of my early expeditions I'd carry Volume I of Service's collected works into the mountains with me to read if stuck in my tent for a few days due to foul weather. They are easy to read, suit my simple brain, youthful sense of humour and love of a good story.

So what you read here (if you get that far) will be more akin to the ballads of Robert Service, the light-hearted verse of Edward Lear, or the tales of Pam Ayres, than to those of Tennyson or Byron and their ilk. But if my words should fail to amuse, you can enjoy the wonderful illustrations of my collaborator, Clare Crooke, at no extra cost.

These verses were written, as you will have gathered from the title of this volume, initially to amuse myself during the Coronavirus lockdown which began in the UK in the spring of 2020. When they heard what I was doing, a few friends asked to see some of the verses. Then my local Neighbourhood Watch co-ordinator asked if he could pass them on with his daily emails. And the next thing I knew I was producing a few verses of nonsense each day which somehow elicited emails from places as far away as Ireland, Scotland and Australia requesting more - which I suggest says as much for the mental condition of those stuck at home during lockdown, as it does for the quality of the rhymes. But hey! – if they bring a smile, I'm happy.

1: The shop around the corner

There's a shop around the corner that I've known for many a year
With every item you could wish, from bread to cans of beer,
There's cold meat, fish and Heinz baked beans and vegetables galore,
Disinfectant, bags of flour and mops to wash the floor.

There's soup and pasta, veggies too, and pills to ease your aches,
And everything that you could need for baking home-made cakes.
There's Kleenex tissues box on box and toilet rolls stacked high,
Just in case disaster strikes and supply chains then run dry.

The man behind the counter has a strangely twisted grin,
He looks as though he's privy to some joke that's just for him;
Some days he'll chew the cud with you for nearly half an hour,
Then stop when someone wants to buy some shampoo for their shower.

In the spring of twenty-twenty a change came to these shores,
A tiny Asian virus put everyone indoors.
Fear then spread from town to town and sent the people wild,
From dear old grey-haired grannies down to the smallest child.

The bug could last for months they said, it's not just like a cold
Protect yourselves and neighbours too, especially the old;
All kissing, handshakes, hugs forbidden, came the grave advice -
But keeping far apart from friends really isn't nice

Someone said 'We're short of grub' and panic then set in,
As the shop around the corner sold out of every tin,
Spaghetti, soups and green-topped milk all vanished from the shelves
When some greedy folk grabbed all they could, to keep just for themselves.

A crafty man who knew the score, said he'd seen panics once before
The one essential for all souls is a cupboard full of toilet rolls.
A single thought now filled each mind: 'Something soft for my behind -
Something I'll need twice a day to keep that nasty bug at bay.'

Have you seen the young mum, with her trolley piled up high
While her toddler sucks a dummy lest she should dare to cry?
Have you seen what she is taking home – just in case?
Sufficient toilet paper for all the human race.

I'm really not facetious, I swear it's not my style,
But thoughtless shoppers just like her remove my every smile.
I only hope one day she suffers no great constipation
For a garage full of toilet rolls will be no consolation.

2: A glass of wine

No glass of wine has touched my lips since Covid reached our shores,
No friendly tap upon my back and the cry – hey friend, what's yours?
No propping up the bar each night, no more the barmaid's smile,
No more her welcome promise of a top-up in a while.

I could do without a whisky, I miss my daily gin,
I'd be happy with a Guinness, but I forgot to get some in.
There's a bottle of brandy on the shelf, its flavour rather good,
But my wife won't let me near it, it's for the Christmas pud.

No glass of wine has touched my lips, I swear that this is true.
That box of chocolate liqueurs? I'm afraid they will not do
My tastes are more refined than that, I'll leave them all alone
And keep them in the larder until my wife comes home.

I'd like to go for supper with a kindly friend or two,
We'd choose a favourite restaurant and a table with a view.
I expect I'd order tender steak and a bottle of house red,
And finish off with something strong when we've all been fed.

I'm desperate for a nightcap to send me off to bed
But make do with a mug of milky Ovaltine instead,
That's how far I've fallen, my life is now a mess
And no-one seems to understand the state of my distress.

So this is what I've come to - don't you think it's rotten?
My daily habits took a dive and now they've reached rock bottom.
No glass of wine has touched my lips, I swear by Aristotle
Since I cannot find the glasses I drink straight from the bottle.

3: Going back to basics

In the spring of twenty-twenty the world was shutting down,
No traffic on the motorways, no-one was left in town,
Alone in isolation the walls were closing in
And every well-used tissue was dropped swiftly in the bin.

With television broken and devices all kaput
The only source of solace could be found inside a book -
An old one full of theories of how life might have been,
When Man emerged from Chimpanzees, stood up and changed the scene.

The trouble with such theories is the way they can't be proved,
For if your fridge is empty you can only think of food,
Food inside your belly, food to keep you warm;
So forget such unproved theories and seek a brighter dawn.

The nights were long and lonely, my thoughts would all run wild,
No logic to this senseless fear, I was tearful as a child.
But the moon was full, as bright as day, it drew me to the door
And then I knew I'd take a risk and break the latest law.

Escape, I cried, though none could hear, I must breathe air again,
I want to see the moonbeams, I want to taste the rain,
I want to go out wandering across the hills and vales,
I want to stand upon a mountain battered by the gales.

This life of isolation is one I'll take no more,
So turned the key, looked left and right, then stepped outside the door.
The street was ghostly silent, no sound from any house,
No black cat mewing with delight as it caught another mouse.

I tiptoed down a country lane that leads into the fields
To brush my hand against a bush and thought how good it feels,
Then barefoot ran through dew-damp grass and knew a surge of joy
And thought no more of viruses, but laughed just like a boy.
IIow good it was to live again, to dance with hands held high

13

No more an eight-foot ceiling, instead a starlit sky.
There was no future locked indoors, from now I would be free
I'd take my chance and roam the world and just see what will be.

The days and weeks rolled into one, the world was mine – all mine
It may have changed, but then I knew that I would be just fine.
I lived on juicy berries and leaves from certain trees,
Healthy and content now, I wandered where I pleased.

My arms were growing stronger, hairs grew on my chest
And here and there when I was tired I'd build a sort of nest,
Then curl up snug just like a babe, make strange sounds when asleep
Never needing that old trick of counting flocks of sheep.

But I was feeling lonely – not much – just now and then
Yet knew there was no mate on earth with whom to share a den,
No woman who would smile at me to make my pulse run wild
Or help to create life again by giving me a child.

A woman? No that thought is wrong, no woman's right for me
There's none I know who'd be prepared to sleep up in a tree.
But then I saw a cheeky Chimp giving me the eye
And knew at once that I had changed enough to make me sigh.

Naked then - but for the mask I wore across my nose,
I saw that I was just like her, no orchid or a rose,
The virus that changed Man for good had been a gift for me,
The book was right, it's time at last to climb back up the tree.

4: A dog's dilemma

When Sandy heard the PM's news he couldn't help but groan,
Confinement's surely not for me, not even in my home.
I need to get my daily dose of non-polluted air
While running free across the fields, racing here and there.

I need to go out walking, at least three times a day,
Watching from a distance all the new born lambs at play.
To play with them would be such fun, of course it's not allowed
But I'm content it must be said, when far from any crowd.

The PM said that we could have each day some exercise.
How long? How far? He didn't say, but hoped that we'd be wise.
Hang on, I thought, we surely need to have more than a clue,
'Cos truth be told I'm sure I need more exercise than you.

I love to roll in smelly mud then wash my coat all clean
By leaping in the current of a clear cold country stream;
I love to chase the rabbits and the squirrels up a tree,
Don't waste your time by throwing balls – you know they're not for me.

But here we are, one walk a day, along a country lane
Where all the other pooches go, every day the same,
There and back, a fringe of grass, a fence to raise my leg at
Can't you see it's boring - I need much more than that.

But Sandy went out walking, of course along the lane
And there discovered dozens more, all with minds the same,
All tugging at their leashes, their owner's arms out straight
Their one intention just to reach the farmer's five-bar gate.

Their masters and their mistresses who'd heard the news before
All knew two metres space between could soon become the law.
So down the lane they went that day, walking one by one
Straining, sniffing, yelping, it was anything but fun.

A big black pooch with yellow teeth had managed to be first,
The others all then got in line, the last place was the worst
And that was Sandy on a lead, he wasn't very happy,
But aloof from all the other dogs, no point in being snappy.

The first one stopped to cock his leg, then wondered where to go,
The queue of mongrels all stopped too, somehow they seemed to know
To keep their social distancing meant dog and master too
Which wouldn't be a problem if there was just a few.

But there were dozens of them, the queue stretched on for miles
Dogs with tongues a-dripping, masters without smiles,
Stopping, starting, sniffing, barking – what a dreadful din -
Sandy had enough of this - his master thought like him.

They ducked beneath a wire fence without the others knowing
Into one big meadow where the springtime grass was growing,
And there he and his master made good their great escape
Away from all the other dogs who'd go just to the gate.

Sandy found his freedom then, he leapt into the air
Then ran around in circles without a single care
Exploring spaces new to him, happy in the clover
Decided he would stay right there, 'til the crisis had passed over.

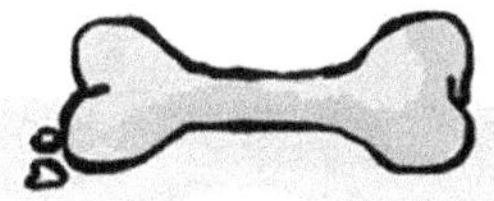

5: Whinge along with me

Four weeks of isolation – or is it only three?
Time has lost its meaning – I'm sure it's not just me,
A week ago last Friday I knew where I was at
But now I've not the foggiest - what d'you think of that?

I no longer know what's right or wrong and wish that I knew better,
I'm a postman in an unknown street who cannot post a letter.
I'm a singer with no song to sing, a gardener with no garden,
A traveller with nowhere to go, a prisoner without a pardon.

I'm Moby Dick - a goldfish, not whale, the Wizard who's forgotten his Oz,
Humpty Dumpty with a fence not a wall - because, because, because...
I can't decide what's up or down, what's back or front or neither,
I'm like the man who's lost a tenner and only found a fiver.

Okay, I guess I've lost the plot, don't say that's nothing new,
But there's something about this madness that will help to see me through.
See me through the weeks to come with a smile upon my face,
No-one to stop me in the street to remind me that I'm a disgrace.

So whinge along with me, I say, give vent to all your madness,
Then try to ignore the way things are and celebrate with gladness.
Life's a laugh if you let it be, it's no good being downhearted,
Today's the best it'll ever be, by tomorrow it will have departed.

6: Time poor

There are brambles on the pathway, ivy up the wall,
The shed that's down the garden can't be seen at all.
I'm told the lawn needs cutting, but to me it looks just fine,
I'll mow it on some sunny day if I can find the time.

The curtains look quite tatty and the pole hangs all askew,
The fixings fell off weeks ago but I don't have a screw.
I'll look for one tomorrow among the grease and grime,
I'd make a start this afternoon, but I don't have the time.

Two cats lie on the sofa, the litter tray's there too,
They look at me with scornful eyes – so what am I to do?
If they'd move off I'd take their place and peacefully recline
But I can't move them - not right now – I simply don't have the time.

My wife would like a pot of tea, or coffee in a cup,
But the crockery we need for that has yet to be washed up,
The bowl is full within the sink, please ignore the slime,
I'll wash it up tomorrow if I can find the time.

The list of jobs goes on and on, I feel defeated by it
Each day it grows much longer, I really can't deny it,
My neighbour's house is spick and span, my wife says it's divine
She'd like ours to be just like that, but I really don't have time.

But now that we're in lockdown, the days are all our own,
No work that we can go to, as we're furloughed here at home,
I'll check that list of jobs again and put them in a line
Then raise my head and pour myself another glass of wine.

7: Lucy

Young Lucy was a dreamer who'd smile throughout the day,
While siblings did their homework, she'd go out to play.
You seldom saw her sitting down, she much preferred to run
Then go to bed exhausted saying, 'Well, now that was fun!'

With Lucy's schooldays over she took the train to town,
But after trying several jobs, she couldn't settle down.
She'd gaze out through the window until the day was done
Then go to bed all wistful, wishing she had had some fun.

When Lucy wore her wedding dress she looked the perfect bride
Standing at the altar, her bridegroom by her side.
Before too long there came the kids, two girls, and then one son
Who gave her lots of pleasure and a huge amount of fun.

As Lucy's kids grew older they began to drift away,
Her husband then was restless and found he couldn't stay
So Lucy took to planning exciting trips to come
For what she really longed for was a life now full of fun.

Lucy rode a camel in a foreign Arab land
With nothing much to look at except the desert sand,
At night the stars were extra bright, by day it was the sun
That scorched the world around her, but brought her lots of fun.

Lucy in the Arctic grew to love the frozen north,
A local man to guide her, one day they both set forth
And saw a baby polar bear playing with its mum
Which Lucy thought endearing, and an awful lot of fun.

Lucy saw big mountains reaching for the sky
So she went mountaineering up where the eagles fly,
And out of dreams to her it seemed her life had just begun
Of all that she'd encountered, this gave the greatest fun.

Now Lucy's old and fragile and in an old folks' home,
She sits there in her armchair reminiscing all alone.
She unpacks all her memories, reveals them one by one
Then whispers with a chuckle – 'Oh my, but that was fun!'

'Hi Gran', said Lucy's daughter's son, 'and how are you today
Have you been exploring in some land that's far away?
Did you see that rainbow painted by the rain and sun?
Did you tell the lovely nurses here it brought you lots of fun?'

Dear Lucy drifted off one day, a smile upon her face;
She'd never wandered far from home, you see she knew her place,
She'd cherished all her daydreams, and now her time had come
Leaving all those memories that might have brought her fun.

8: The cuckoo

I thought I heard a cuckoo call at five past three today,
If so, he's back from Africa – and that's a long, long way.
A long way over land and sea, for days upon the wing,
However does he do it – and then have breath to sing?

It's not a song of beauty, but it's good enough for me,
It makes me think of spring-times when I was fancy free,
Free to stroll among the trees and watch the leaves unfurl
When I was but a country lad and you were still a girl.

The fragrance of the woodland flowers, a sea of vivid blue,
Picnics on our favourite hill with uninterrupted view,
The stars at night, the full moon bright, their glory never dims
When walking on a lonely beach, planning midnight swims.

Young we were and innocent, our days were full of fun,
No cares would come to bother us, no clouds would hide our sun,
We thought today was all there is, why worry for tomorrow?
No tears, no fears, we let them pass, we had no time for sorrow.

But that was then and this is now, and only Man has changed
The world out there is still as grand, it's just been rearranged;
Don't listen to the pessimists and all they have to say
Just look around and count the blessings you've received today.

You'll find there are so many more than you had ever thought
And every one more precious than the costliest thing you've bought,
So step outside and close your eyes and it's possible you may
Hear a cuckoo calling you back from Africa today.

9: Great grandpa

Great Grandpa's face was strangely square,
Lots of flesh,
Little hair.
Tufts that sprouted from his ears
Had not been trimmed for many years,
Eyes that gazed out into space
In memory of some distant place
Or some sweet girl he used to know
Who left him, oh so long ago.
His teeth? he never had a lot
But kept his dentures in a pot,
Then scared me sometimes with his grin

When he forgot to put them in.
His brow was furrowed into lines,
His nose the colour of red wines.
He'd fought his way through two World Wars
And lost a leg on foreign shores,
After that he wore a peg
And lodged it down his trouser leg.

Great Grandpa gave no thought to clothes -
Where his came from, well, no-one knows.
Tatty shirt and tea-stained vest,
With trousers pulled up to his chest.
His army boots stomped on the floor;
A sound I'll not hear any more.
The old man seldom comes to mind,
There's nothing much to say
Yet banishing his memory
Has a price to pay.
It's years since I last thought of him
But in a dreamy haze
I wiped the bathroom mirror
And - oh was I amazed!
For as the razor scraped my chin
Discovered I look just like him.

10: Grumpy Joe

The teenage sons of Grumpy Joe upped and left him years ago,
His constant moaning brought them low, that moody, gloomy so and so.
Then his wife of twenty years had just about enough
So one day grabbed her handbag, and then left in a huff.

He took retirement early, his colleagues were relieved,
Glad to see the back of him, the way that he deceived
Each of the men he worked with at one time or another,
He'd even left the union 'cos someone called him Brother.

So there he was, a grumpy man who had no friends to see him,
A prisoner of his making, no-one but he could free him.
His house was old and dusty, like Joe it looked forlorn,
But then you must remember how it echoed with his scorn.

Joe never watched the tele, never listened to the news,
Said it's full of speculation, not much more than pundits' views.
He wouldn't read the papers, said they're just a waste of space
Despising tabloid editors as a national disgrace.

There was no pleasing Grumpy Joe, I think I've made that clear,
He had no hidden attributes, like Scrooge of yesteryear.
He threw away the telephone, never used the post
But worst of all the internet is what he hated most.

One day he found his local shop had nothing on display,
All the shelves were empty, but why? He couldn't say.
The cashier looked exhausted as she wiped away a tear,
And said there might be no more stock for at least another year.

Joe looked out through his window at the old familiar street
And noted only silence and the slap of joggers' feet.
There were no speeding motorists, of whom he could complain,
No buses passing to and fro, no sound of distant train.

Some strangers went by walking, each one with a hound
And with lots of space between them they didn't make a sound.
How odd, he thought, there's something wrong this town is not the same,
Then scratched his head and tried to think of someone he could blame.

The days turned into weeks that passed him by without a word,
But through the eerie silence he began to hear a bird
A bird that sang so sweetly from a neighbour's maple tree
He thought for just a moment: 'he could be singing just for me.'

Such thoughts did not come easy to this moody so and so,
But day by day the heart was melting inside Grumpy Joe.
He'd go into the garden he'd neglected all those years
And find the song so blissful he was often drawn to tears.

The bird's song changed an old man's mood from gloom to open-hearted
And made him think of better days and those from whom he'd parted,
So there and then he made a vow to smile because he could,
And every day he'd find a way to do someone some good.

So if Coronavirus begins to get you down
Don't snap at those you really love, or wear a constant frown,
Just think of all the good things that you're blessed with every day
And let the joy of birdsong chase those dreary blues away.

11: Confusion

Does anyone know what today is,
The truth is, I don't have a clue;
Is it Tuesday, Friday or Sunday?
I've no idea – have you?

Any idea what the time is?
My clock gave up long ago,
Daybreak or dusk I'm really confused
While the sun is still lying low.

I cannot guess what the month is,
Is it March, April, May or perhaps June?
Is it time to start planning for Christmas,
Or is that a little too soon?

If it's daybreak I'll throw back the duvet
And slide wearily out of my bed,
I'll stagger into the bathroom –
If it's Thursday I'll then wash my head.

But if today is Tuesday
There's something I must do
It's the day to put our bin bags out -
I will, but what about you?

As for the month, I really am lost
Each day the sky is cloud-free,
If it's spring or summer I couldn't care less
Whatever will be will be.

But when this crisis is over
And our lives resume their routine,
We'll look on these days of confusion
As a time when we lived in a dream.

For now I'll enjoy bewilderment,
It's a condition that suits me just fine.
There's nothing I need to do right now
So I'll sit back and then bide my time.

12: Stuff

'Now look', she said, 'it's time to make some sense of all this clutter,
Don't look at me with those sad eyes, say 'yes dear', don't just mutter
You've no more work to go to, and no work means no stress
So let's have no excuses, and we will clear this mess.'

'Okay', said I, 'but not just me for you must play your part
If I'm to suffer, so must you, so where d'you think we'll start?'
'I will take the records and you must throw some books,'
'Some books?' said I, 'oh, surely not!' - then gave one of my looks.

'You've more books than my records, so more to throw away,
If you could read them all again, that's ten at least each day,
But music's rather different, it soothes the saddest heart
And lifts us with such joyfulness and fills each lonely part.

'But still I know it must be done, we owe it to the kids
For when we turn our toes up they'll be grateful that we did,
Grateful that we threw a load of rubbish in a skip,
So let us make a start right now - just take a lucky dip.'

She spread the records on the floor and sat right down beside them.
She stacked them into ten neat piles and then began to file them;
Rock and folk and jazz times two and some by J.S. Bach,
Each one full of memories to warm a woman's heart.

Our house is full of books you know, they're piled up on the floor
There's not much room to store them so I won't buy any more.
Yet each one is a loyal friend I could not be without
They've seen me through some tough times, of that there is no doubt.

There are books by Ernest Hemingway, books by Robert Graves,
Travel books all battered that have seen some better days.
There are tales from Robert Service with his ballads from the north
I once stuffed into my rucksack as a young man setting forth.

Each one is like my family, to dump them would be cruel
There's surely space to keep some (I'm a sentimental fool)
If music means as much to you, each record in its sleeve
Reminds you of our children, well that's what I believe.

So here we are, just you and me faced with a dilemma
What to do with all this stuff if we're to stay together?
'Don't be daft', she told me, 'it's surely not a sin
To keep the best but drop the rest straight into the bin!'

The moral of this story is you do not need a lot
To make you really happy if you value what you've got,
So sort out all your records and all the books you own,
Get rid of 'stuff' if possible, then make your house a home.

13: The nightingale's cure

Don't speak to me of lockdown while my windows have no bars
Just leave me to the moonbeams and a heaven full of stars,
I'll give myself to silences, but should their magic fail
I'll sell my soul to the sacred hymn sung by the nightingale.

When I grew up an Essex lad I lived near woodland trees,
There were no 'Keep Out' notices, so rambled where I pleased
In summer and in springtime, on still nights and in gales
I'd take the dog and wander off to hear the nightingales.

Their song still sends a tingle throughout my ageing spine,
It's far more beneficial than a glass of sparkling wine.
I drink its healing wholesomeness and then come back for more
Knowing what a perfect cure the nightingale's singing for.

One spring I walked the North Downs Way, it took me seven days
From Farnham round to Dover on leafy green byeways.
I stopped to have my picnic in a sheltered woodland shaw.
And was serenaded by a song I'd heard some years before.

It was, of course, a nightingale, singing just for me,
So sweet, so pure, I lost all interest in my flask of tea.
I sat there on a lichened log as tears ran down my cheek
And swore I'd stay there all alone – at least until next week.

So speak no more of lockdown while my windows have no bars
I'll surrender to the moonbeams and a heaven full of stars,
And no matter what the future holds I'm certain of one thing
Year on year we'll all rejoice to hear the nightingale sing.

14: I know my place

You should see my wife in the garden
Daring the weeds to grow,
She'll grab something green from the border
And cry: 'Gotcha, you so and so!'

She's out there at this moment
Down on her knees on the lawn,
She's probably drying the grasses out
That were damp with dew from the dawn.

She plays tug-o-war with a blackbird,
No rope – but a long juicy worm.
There's never but one certain winner,
Wouldn't you think that she would learn?

She knows every plant's botanical name
They're all engraved in her head,
But I'm banned from even breathing near them
For fear they'll end up dead.

If she spends too long in the greenhouse
She grows an inch or more,
Was a time when she was shorter than me
But now she's six feet four.

Now I confess that I'm no gardener,
I don't know my clay from my loam,
But I love the peace and the harmony
That makes our garden a home.

I'd do my best but my best is no good,
As a gardener I'm a dead loss,
So I'll do what every poor man should do
And accept that my wife is the boss.

15: When it's all over

When this pandemic is over I'm going to let down my hair,
I'll throw every item of clothing off
And run down the High Street all bare.

It's time that I did something crazy, of course it's not really me,
But I'm fed up with Man-made convention
And want to be totally free.

When all this nonsense is over, I'll do whatever I like
I'll climb on my roof in the darkness
And pretend I'm an owl in the night.

Once this virus leaves us, I'll take a long walk in the rain,
I'll roll down a hill in the moonlight,
Then do it all over again.

My wife reckons I'm going crazy, and you know, that's probably true,
For the older I get I'm willing to bet
She's right - I'm going cuckoo.

My dad always said I'm a dreamer, he'd be shaking his head in despair
If he knew I'd gone bonkers in lockdown
And pull out each strand of his hair.

I'm sorry, I'd say, that's just how I am, I've had it right up to here,
I fear one more month will defeat me,
Already it seems like a year.

A year, did I say? It's time I confessed to the thoughts
that come into my head,
They arrive in the night and try as I might
They're still there when I leave my bed.

If you knew what those curious thoughts were, you'd look at me in disdain,
You'd say the old boy has gone ga-ga
And vow never to greet me again.

But when this pandemic is over, you'll be crazy as me, I will bet,
So let's have a neighbourhood party
And see how daft we can get.

16: Looking for swifts

I went into the garden and looked up to the sky
Hoping the first of this year's swifts would soon come racing by
I want to hear that screeching sound emitted from their beaks,
Tho' their song is really not a song, just a lot of shrieks.
Shrieks? well yes, I guess they are but they can be forgiven,
Angels' arrows, fast as lightning, gifts it seems from heaven.

The same birds come back every year and each year fly away,
Truth be told they'd please me best if they would only stay,
But hating our damp winters, they need sub-Saharan sun
To guide them over Africa, the adults with their young.
So in our dying summers they gather on the wires
Then fly off to the sunny south fulfilling their desires.

No swifts are in the sky today, I hope they won't be long
But until they are I'll be content to hear the blackbird's song,
He may be rather plain to see, but oh my! what a sound,
He comes into our garden, his ear cocked to the ground
Listening for worms, I think, perhaps with young to feed
Leaving all the blue tits to fill themselves with seed.

The songthrush and the tiny wren are favourites of mine
They wake me up each morning and sing til supper time.
The raucous rook and hooded crow, they croak on treetop branches,
The pheasant breaking cover when he hears a man's advances,
But now we're into springtime and the first warm, sunny weeks
It's the swifts that I am longing for with their excited shrieks.

17: A turn around the garden

I'll just take a turn round the garden
Before I have my tea,
The missus usually hands me a cuppa
Out there at half past three.

The garden, it ain't very big you know
Just a dozen paces by ten,
A circuit takes less than a minute
Before I walk around it again.

The views, they're somewhat restricted,
I can't see over the fence,
But the flowers my missus has planted
Are beginning to make some sense.

There are bluebells filling one corner,
Lavender creeps to the door,
A clematis climbs up the drainpipe -
I'm not sure that's what drainpipes are for!

So I'll make my afternoon circuit
And see what I can find.
You're welcome to come and join me,
But you'll have to walk behind.

Ten circuits will make my head spin
But they keep me fit as a flea,
At least that is what I tell my wife
When she brings me my cup of tea.

There's a trench appearing in the lawn,
Perhaps I should change my route
To even the surface of once-lush turf
Now scarred by a size ten boot.

But first I'll sit with my PG Tips,
No fancy Earl Grey for me;
A chocolate digestive would go down well
If I can dunk it in my tea.

Then I'll dream of other walks I made
In the weeks before lockdown,
Walks on hills so far away
From any slumbering town.

Walks on winding footpaths,
Walks along country lanes,
Walks among distant mountains
With unpronounceable names.

There were fun-filled walks with the family
When both our girls were small,
We'd pitch our tent in a meadow
And listen to raindrops fall.

Walking's in our genes I guess,
It's always been the same.
I'd rather be out walking
Than in here with a silly board game.

Oh dear, I'm getting all wistful,
The wife says I'm becoming a pain,
So I'll finish my well-earned refreshment
And take a turn round the garden again.

18: To speak of snails and slimy things

It's hardly rained since lockdown began, I'd forgotten how fresh it can feel
But letting it dampen my upturned face assures me that this is real.
Lying awake an hour before dawn I knew outside it was raining,
A grin then stretched from ear to ear, there's no way
that I'd be complaining.
I'm not so sure about my wife – for although her garden has needs
She knows it takes only a cupful of rain to bring up a bucket of weeds.

Weeds she can handle when down on her knees, poking along the border,
With never a scowl but a twist of the trowel everything's kept in order,
But across the path a tramline tells of something we've not seen for ages,
A slug or a snail whose silvery trail will ignite my wife's inner rages.
Where do they hide when the sun shines? That's what I'd like to know.
Where do they go in the wintertime when it's cold enough to snow?

Now that it's spring and our feathered friends sing,
just give us an hour's worth of rain,
And they'll all appear like they did last year and cause havoc all over again.
'Oh those slimy creatures!' I hear my poor wife moan
'Be careful not to step on them or you'll take them into our home.'
But leave them to their own devices will only make things worse
For her cherished hostas when slimy are guaranteed to make her curse.

I've seen her jumping up and down and pulling at her hair,
Raging at the slugs and snails she said should not be there.
But then she had a bright idea and called her favourite thrush,
'Slugs and snails for breakfast' she cried, 'Come now, but please don't rush
There's enough for you and your feathered friends,
and I really don't want to boast
But I think you'll find them more to your taste than
a plateful of beans on toast.'

With a tap-tap here and a tap-tap there,
empty shells lay glist'ning with dew
But there's nothing left for the hedgehog to eat -
we'd forgotten he likes the slugs too.
You may not think they'd do much good,
and my wife would say you're right
But slugs and snails and slimy things feed creatures of the night
So next time you see a slug on the path don't step on it with your shoe
Just think of Nature's intricate web, and imagine that slug could be you.

19: Books to see me through

Lockdown's not been bad for me, I really must confess
I've found so many gems of old once buried in the mess,
The mess that is my office where I spend much of the day
In peaceful meditation (at least that's what I say).
That's my excuse to close the door lest any noise intrude,
I wouldn't like my wife to think that I was being rude.
Truth to tell I've all I need to keep the blues away
Except perhaps some records, but they're kept downstairs to play.
It's books that keep me chipper, that bring a smile or two,
Some that I'd not read for years so now seem just like new.
There are novels by a friend of mine who's living far away,
Each page is reminiscent of the things he used to say.
There are books that make me wistful of the time when they were bought,
Books I found too heavy with deep depressing thought,
Books that make me laugh out loud and some to make me groan
With the loss of folk I used to know who stayed with us at home.
There's poetry in covers that signify a dream,

A few are so pretentious I feel that I could scream
But others I could quote for hours, each stanza like a song
They've travelled with me everywhere, I tell you, they belong.
There are picture books of mountains in remote exotic places,
Himalayan valleys with friendly Sherpa faces.
Those distant lands come back to me, they'll never go away
As long as travel writers have something fresh to say.
Like tales of great adventure that are piled up on my shelf,
I couldn't part with any I selected for myself,
Some are first editions I was invited to review,
Some are old and battered – were they ever new?
My desk holds several volumes that are marked to read again,
Some have home-made wrappers to hide a coffee stain.
There are lines I've annotated that make me wish that I
Had talent like the author's, but whose skills have passed me by.
So I'll sit here in my office filled with other people's words
And make the most of lockdown like those who study birds.

20: Rich man, poor man

The world is your oyster, I once heard it said,
And you can fit the whole universe inside your head.
You can travel all day without leaving your home
And be the richest of men with no wealth of your own.

Don't cover your walls with the works of Van Gogh
Or hoard all your treasures upstairs in your loft.
Don't covet the homes of a smug billionaire
Or waste breath complaining 'life just isn't fair.'

No, life isn't fair, it's not fair at all,
But remember the rich have the farthest to fall.
Those with the most have much more to lose,
And the biggest mistakes made by those who can choose.

Now poverty's tough when you've little to eat
And the pavement is cold with no shoes on your feet.
I think of the homeless whose lost pleading eyes
Express what lies hidden by unspoken cries.

Between those extremes there stand most of us,
Pigs in the middle, we're the ones who will fuss
As we envy the grass that is green o'er the fence.
But envy is shameful; it doesn't make sense

There'll always be someone who has more than you,
While standing behind you there'll be a long queue.
It just goes to show that those who have more
Are poor men with money, while the rich could be poor.

21: Feeling kinda peckish

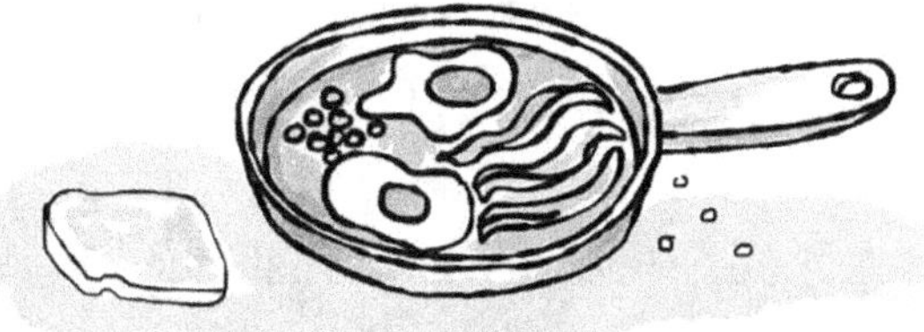

I've barely stopped eating since lockdown began,
My wife says I'm putting on weight,
I begin with an early pre-breakfast snack
And continue all day 'til it's late.

Bacon and eggs and a tin of baked beans
And a couple of tasty hot dogs,
Keep me on track 'til I'm peckish again
When I could eat a bucket of frogs.

A packet of chocolate digestive
Helps my mid-morning coffee go down,
Then a light snack of something quite tasty
From the delicatessen in town.

Lunch is a bowl of soup or two
And maybe a poached egg on toast,
Then a box or more of Walker's crisps
Lest I should fade away like a ghost.

Cake goes down well with my afternoon tea –
Black Forest Gateau is best,
Then a Mars Bar, a Kit-Kat or something like that
While I take my pre-dinner rest.

Plenty of carbohydrates will do
Washed down with a bottle of wine,
Don't bother with any of your fancy cuisine
Just pile it up, I'll be fine.

Alka Seltzer is what I shall need
To prepare my belly for bed,
Then I'll collapse in a heap so exhausted,
My wife will fear that I'm dead.

I'm afraid to go out of the house now,
Not even into the street,
My stomach is so extended these days
It's months since I last saw my feet.

I can't wear the shirts that I used to,
My trousers are now much too tight,
To pull on a vest or my underpants
Involves an incredible fight.

The seams of my jacket have all torn apart,
I guess it's because of the strain.
Perhaps I should lose some weight then,
So I can wear it again.

Yes! It's time I cut down on my eating
So I'll submit myself to a diet,
In fact I'll start in the morning -
After breakfast will be a good time to try it.

22: Now and then

In days of old when the weak were bold
And the stars danced rings round the sky,
Rabbits could talk and fishes would walk
And the seas were all desert dry.

Cats in the dark would wake up and bark
To deaden the mewing of dogs,
While up in the trees were roots and not leaves
Where nightingales croaked like frogs.

Back then I'd walk and only talk
If there was something I needed to say,
I had no end of jolly good friends
With whom to work and play.

I'd sing with joy like an innocent boy
And speak not one unkind word.
I was sober and sane, with nothing to gain
By being cynical or absurd.

Well, that was then, they said it would end
If it wasn't already too late,
But I said I'd resist, I'd try to exist
If adulthood could wait.

So forgive me if I'm just an eedjut
Who makes not one jot of sense,
I'd rather be thought slightly crazy
Than complain or sit on the fence.

In these days of Coronavirus
It's too easy to be brought down low,
So I jump out of bed every morning
And watch the sun rise with a glow.

That sun and the blue sky behind it
Are gifts that will make me feel glad
And banish all sorrows before they begin
As they did when I was a lad.

They say I'm no longer a young lad,
I'm craggy, bearded and grey
But deep down my heart is just as it was
When a dreamer, just yesterday.

23: Sleepless nights

I'm bleary-eyed this morning, I hardly slept a wink,
And when staring at the ceiling nights are longer than you think.
I've been doing mathematics and counting flocks of sheep
And thought of all the books I've read as I tried to get to sleep.

The hours crept by so slowly, one second at a time,
I thought I'd make a cup of tea or drink a glass of wine,
I tossed and turned this way and that, got tangled in the sheets
While the lonely hours turned into days, and days turned into weeks.

If I'm grumpy over breakfast I hope you'll bear with me
I'll try to keep my temper – but we will have to see
If a bowl of lumpy porridge will bring me back to life
And make me sympathetic to my ever-patient wife.

'What's that?' she scoffed, 'you try to tell me that you've had no rest
I can't believe you're serious – is this some kind of jest?
Last night your eyes were barely closed when you were well away,
It was I who turned the light out, and I who had to say

Goodnight my dear, sleep well my love, like every other night
No! You were busy snoring with all your blessed might!
The windows starting rattling, there was trembling from the floor,
There was banging on the bedroom wall from folk who live next door.

I've not heard such a racket, not a man-made sound so loud
Since caught in London's traffic with a rowdy football crowd.
Don't say you've had a sleepless night, I know that isn't true
In fact, I swear I've had at least eight hours less than you.'

'Ha!' I said (my blood was up) – does she have no shame?
How dare she look me in the eyes and say that I'm to blame?
I checked my watch beside the bed, studied it - and then
Noticed it said eight o'clock – that's eight o'clock pm!

It seemed I'd slept around the clock, and not been wide awake
So put my dentures in my mouth and confessed to my mistake.
'I'm sorry dear,' I grovelled, 'forgive me one more time
I'll try to be more thoughtful – for snoring's such a crime.

I'll try to keep my mouth shut when I go to bed.
I'll try to learn a lesson from a book that I once read,
It said don't go too early, but sit up 'til it's late
And let your wife sleep for you, while you stay wide awake.'

24: Hope

If you've started to chew on the woodwork
To allay every one of your fears,
If your hair's now so long and tangled
You've attacked it with garden shears.
If you yearn for something quite different
Away from your household chores,
And you've cleaned every part of the kitchen,
The cupboards, the windows, the floors
Then all that is left – and it's surely the best
Like a bath full of bubbly soap,
Is to immerse yourself in the luxury
Of that sweet-smelling promise called hope.

If the children are running you ragged
And you've been driven mad by their noise,
If you're wishing you had a few goldfish
Instead of two girls and three boys;
If you've lost every one of your childhood dreams

And your adult face fills with frowns,
I suggest you find peace in the garden -
At least 'til the sun goes down.
Out there I swear the sweet fresh air
Will enable you to cope
With all the problems you'd otherwise face
If it hadn't been for hope.

Hope can be likened to sunrise,
It says there are good things ahead
It'll be many more hours til it goes down again,
So wake up and get out of bed.
You'll find that the day's full of promise,
There are so many good things to do,
Don't lie there and stare at the ceiling
It doesn't give much of a view.
Imagine instead, once you're out of your bed,
You're in love and about to elope,
It will start your day in a joyful way
And all because of hope.

25: Once upon a time

Whatever happened to yesterday? It was surely not that long ago
I remember it ever so clearly, just ask me if you'd like to know.
Why opt for Now when the past was so good,
there was so much we had to enjoy,
When you were a wee girl in pigtails and I was a knobbly-kneed boy.

Roy Rogers my cowboy hero, had teeth unbelievably white,
He'd chase all the baddies out of the town, at five o'clock each Friday night.
Bill and Ben came before him, they were flower pot men with a weed.
Our tele like others was just black and white, but that was all we'd need.

When yobs dodged their National Service, they'd become
Teddy Boys instead,
With brothel creepers on their feet, and Brylcream rubbed over the head.
Shops closed at midday on Wednesday, the banks locked
their doors at three,
Fish and chips were one and six, so we'd have them for our tea.

Buses all had conductors, 'Clippies' we called them then,
Some were stern-faced women, but most were grumpy old men.
Smokers would sit on the upper deck, with Woodbines
draped from their lips,
Others would cram below the stairs and stand if nowhere to sit.

Supermarkets didn't exist, there were food shops all in a line,
Queues would form at each counter, but we somehow had the time.
Manual workers did five and a half days, typists worked nine to five,
Nobody worked on a Sunday, the 'wealthy' would go for a drive.

When you went for a walk you'd look all around to
enjoy the peaceful scene,
Unlike today when everyone's eyes are glued to a Smartphone screen.
There were no such things as computers, no iPads or gizmos like that,
We'd never heard of obesity, you were either thin or fat.

I know you will say I'm a Luddite, and with that I have to agree,
But forgive my dreamy nostalgia,
you'll be the same when you're old like me.
The past was such a joyful place, the sun shone all the time
And I live each day all over again when I open a bottle of wine.

26: Only a statistic

Two legs, two arms, one heart, one head,
Two eyes, one voice, with words unsaid,
One cherished life now sorely missed,
Not just a number on a list.

Statistics tumbling from the news
Are cast aside like worn-out shoes.
Figures told by po-faced men,
Show rising lines that have no end.

Cold numbers increase by the day,
Computers have no words to say.
Lists of figures soon depart,
Statistics with no beating heart.

Next time you hear these numbers
Remember what they mean,
To those who've lost a loved-one
And now have shattered dreams.

A father, mother, sibling,
A neighbour, long-lost friend,
Loved at their beginning
And loved too, at their end.

Think of gifts they'd love to give
If just a few more years to live,
And remember, one non-beating heart
Is NOT a statistic on a chart.

27: Something's not quite right

I've got the eebie-jeebies, I fear there's something wrong
Was it something that I ate last night – some food we'd had too long?
It's not just wind, I'm sure of that, and I couldn't say it's pain,
But it bubbles up inside of me – oops! there it goes again.

I ask my wife if she's okay. She claims to feel alright,
But I'm really not the ticket, for I had a rotten night.
I dreamed I had a fever and woke up in a sweat,
My eyes are glazed, my face is white, my wife says 'Don't you fret.'

Perhaps an Alka Seltzer will get me on my feet
And an after-breakfast toddle a short way down our street.
Outside? Oh no! I felt deep down a rising sense of panic
I'd forgotten for a moment this grim world-wide pandemic.

Nine weeks we've been in lockdown, I can't take any more.
Nine weeks of isolation behind our closed front door.
Nine weeks, so says my diary, even the weather's not the same,
Nine weeks of brilliant sunshine with hardly any rain.

You know those eebie-jeebies I spoke of at the start
They're not down in my belly, but gathered round my heart
There are no pills to cure my ills, no surgeon with his knife
But an end of this darn virus, so I can get on with my life.

28: Why me?

Do you get up some mornings, still scratching at your head
Thinking you're off colour and then go back to bed?
Is your tongue all thick and furry, and not as it should be
And wonder why you feel like that and ask yourself – why me?

Have you ever been an angler in water to your knees
In a quiet country river among the willow trees,
While a wriggling, gasping, spotted trout is trying to break free,
Before gazing with a pleading eye as if to say, why me?
Have you stood upon a harbour wall when trawlers came ashore,
Their nets so full and bulging, no room for any more
Fishes by the thousand snatched from a foreign sea
Destined for some diner's meal, no voice to ask why me?
Have you wandered through a woodland when the birds began to sing?
Have you seen the woodman lift his axe and marvelled at its swing?
Have you seen the blackbird's nest up high, falling from the tree
And heard a clutch of nestlings cry: now hold on please - why me?
D'you ever wonder what it's like to be a well-bred horse
Racing in the 'National' on Aintree's famous course,
You're at the front, a furlong left, chased by another three
While the crowd is going crazy, and you think, 'ang on, why me?

No. You and I are human, our minds don't work that way
Or else we'd change the way we live, beginning with today.
But we're smug with satisfaction at all the things we've got
And never stop to ask why me? Instead we think - why not!

29: What if?

I don't have much time for 'if-onlys' when related to the past,
What once was done can't be undone, say sorry and move on fast.
What if? I consider quite different, it can help you get ahead,
Being a spur for tomorrow, showing which path you should tread.
What if? kick-starts your planning, gives strength to handle the strain,
It picks you up when you've fallen, and helps you try once again.
What if? I had my brother's brain, and the skills he has in each hand,
Or my mother's gift for music, I'd play guitar in a rock n'roll band.
What if? I looked like a film star, my handsome face on the screen,
Wherever I went I'd be happy to hear the sound of my fans' joyful scream.
What if? the millionaire's daughter agreed to become my wife
I'd never need to work again, I'd be rich for the rest of my life.
What if? – I said in my dreams last night,
while my beloved was still wide awake,
Then opened my eyes to see her scowl – I knew then I'd made a mistake.
'What if? – you bone-idle dreamer', her face pressed close to my head
'What if you did something useful for once,
and brought me my breakfast in bed.'

30: Four legs and a tail

I've long had a passion for animals that began when I was a boy,
When I'd much rather have a pet to look after than any expensive toy.
It all began with a hamster with a cute adorable face,
I took it to the village show but lost it in a race.
The guinea pig Mum gave me next ran riot around the house
Then caused too much confusion when it mated with a mouse.
I was given a colourful parrot, complete with cage and a perch,
But as soon as my girlfriend heard it swear, she left me in the lurch.
When Mum and Dad both passed away, I remained in the family home
But without their cheerful chatter it was empty and I was alone,
So I thought I'd have a pet or two to give me some company,
A dog at my feet, some fish in a bowl, a cat curled up on my knee.
But of course they soon took over, I was much too soft I confess,
And almost before I knew it I was knee deep in their mess.
Now, a badger digs holes in the garden, a fox sits tight in my chair
There's a pile of bills I owe to my vet, and litter trays everywhere.
Squirrels took over the attic, mice run all over the floor,
While one of my favourite tortoises attempts to push open the door.
Tadpoles squirm in the kitchen sink, frogs swim in my bath,
Canaries sit on the curtain poles where their antics make me laugh.
But there's nowhere left for me to sit, nowhere for me to sleep,
The table is cluttered with animals, there's no place where I can eat.
One thing I haven't mentioned, and that's the dreadful pong,
My neighbours moan about it, they tell me it is wrong.
But as I say, I'm a softie, the animals always come first,
Four legs and a tail, a slug and a snail, there's not one I would curse.
So as they've taken up residence, with no room in the house for me
I've built for myself a hideaway, halfway up a tree.

31: One thing after another

Wake up! Wake up!' my dear wife said,
'There's lots to do – get out of bed.
I've made a list of jobs for you,
They'll take a while to work right through.
First get up and wash your face,
The bathroom's clear, there's lots of space
To clean your teeth and brush your hair
That's growing wild just everywhere.
Then go downstairs, make cups of tea,
Breakfast next – save some for me,
A bowl of cornflakes, slice of toast
Well, maybe two, but that's the most,
And when you've done the washing up
And put away each plate and cup
Go out, and if the weather's fine
Hang the washing on the line.
Next, clean the windows, Hoover floors,

Dust the bookcase, wipe the doors.
Take magazines that come each day,
And those we've read just throw away.
I want the house all spic and span
To suit the person that I am.
I know that seems I'm rather proud
But a cluttered house is not allowed.

Now that's done, you take the lead,
Check the fridge, see what we need.
Be sure you write each item down
Then catch the morning bus to town.
Make certain that you're back for lunch
But if you're early, we'll have brunch...'

'Hold on a mo,' I tried to say,
'That's quite a lot for half a day.
Trapped at home's a bad idea,
I prefer the office to being here.'
And can you guess what she then said?
'Oh stop complaining, come back to bed!'

32: The cottage gardener

There's a cottage with a garden overhung by graceful trees
Where lives an old grey-headed man, content and at his ease,
His days are filled with labour in the garden he adores
And not just for the way it keeps him busy out of doors.

His days start mostly early when the sun begins to rise,
Then stands outside his kitchen rubbing sleep from out his eyes.
He makes himself a mug of tea and listens to the birds
Whose chorus at this time of day says more than any words.

He'll wander round the garden with the dew still on the grass
Planning what to do today, not thinking of the past.
A gardener in his garden's never short of things to do
And seldom finds the time to stand and look out at the view.

Though no-one else lives with him he is happy on his own
For Mother Nature's children all make sure he's not alone,
There are rabbits and grey squirrels, sometimes a fallow deer
Not to mention all the songbirds he's always thrilled to hear.

They tiptoe through the garden, yet never trample on his plot
For they know he'll share with others all the veggies that he's got,
The runner beans and lettuce, the spuds and Brussels sprouts,
Are what he leaves for neighbours when he knows that they are out.

There are old folk in the village who'd appreciate some more,
So he takes a bag of fruit or veg and hangs it from their door.
There is no note or card inside of things he'd like to say
It's just a gesture of his kindness, with nowt for them to pay.

I met him once, long years ago, he was ancient even then,
Eighty years his age I guess, the gentlest of all men.
He showed me round his garden then we shared a pot of tea
And sat among the honeysuckle listening to the bees.

A quiet man, I saw at once he's one who clearly cares,
A single man who never envies those who live in pairs,
His contentment is enhanced I'm sure by all the things he grows
While his smiling eyes reflect the beauty of his finest rose.

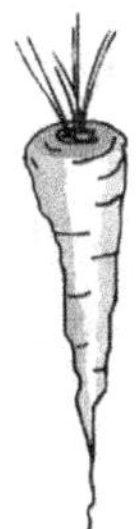

33: What happens when you croak?

I threw back my head to sing last night, but all that came out was a croak.
I tried it again but it sounded the same, I imagined it was some kind of joke.
So I gargled a glass of salt water, then spat it out down the drain,
But when I attempted to sing once more the sound was exactly the same.

There was nothing about it that pleased me, it even annoyed the cat
Who curled his lip and arched his back and scraped his claws on the mat.
The parrot looked down from his lofty perch with eyes that suggested fear,
Then squawked 'What's going on down there –
what's that horrible sound I hear?'

I was feeling pretty depressed by now as I climbed up on my chair,
For when I went to scratch my beard I found I had no hair.
My skin felt so strange, so different, it was never like this before,
And I left some curious footprints when I hopped across the floor.

I saw a few flies on the ceiling then, a group of two or three,
So opened my mouth and shot out my tongue and had them for my tea.
I knew now my life would be different, but hoped it was some kind of game
As my cat fled into the garden then stared through the window pane.

There's a pond out in the garden with lily pads round the side,
I fancied going out there at once, then into the water I'd slide.
Some big poppy eyes winked at me, and a mouth stretched wide in a grin
Then a croaking voice seduced me, 'Come join me and have a swim.'

It was lovely in the water with tadpoles everywhere
Were they mine? I wondered. If so I ought to care,
But a burning touch came on my cheek, so surprising it made me wince,
Then I opened one eye when I heard my wife cry:
'Wake up my handsome prince!'

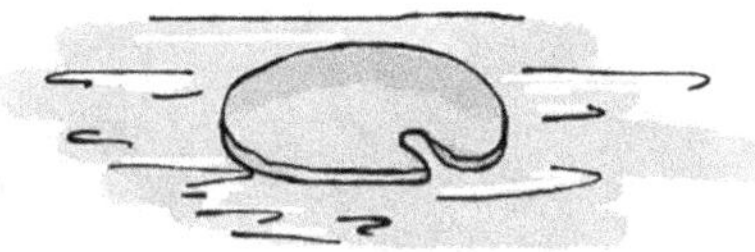

34: Forty winks

Half an hour in the afternoon, when I've had something to eat
Will set me up for the rest of the day and put me on my feet,
Half an hour, that's all it takes to face the day anew,
But it all depends, of course, what my wife wants me to do.

My mother needed forty winks, my dad could cope with ten,
But he'd give a sly wink and whisper: 'that's the thing about men!'
I can see them now in the parlour, stretched out on a favourite chair,
My mum looking neat and dainty, but dad with his feet in the air.

With heads thrown back, they'd be off in a tick, each with tightly shut eyes,
But mouths would open down to their chins as if they were catching flies.
They both could snore for England, gold medal winners for sure,

The windows would rattle (so would their teeth) til the neighbours
beat on the door.

They were the loving-most parents a boy could have,
I swear that they were the best,
And I tell you all this not to darken their names but to get it off my chest.
You see their need of an afternoon doss they've passed right down to me,
And I picture them now in heaven looking down with a sense of glee.

I think now and then they're having a joke when asleep in Dad's old chair,
For a sound disturbs me at the door but I find that no-one's there.
Another time the phone will ring and I'll stumble to my feet,
Only to find it's the ice cream man just outside in the street.

Half an hour in the afternoon, that's surely not much to ask.
Half an hour to digest my food, and then you can set me a task.
Half an hour on the sofa, or half an hour on the bed,
But take my toes-up away from me and I might as well be dead.

So if you're looking down on me Dad, and Mum's up there with you too
I want you to know that I've mastered your trick of knowing what to do.
Should someone disturb my afternoon kip, I'll treat it just like a crime,
I'll throw back my head and open my mouth and
snore much louder next time.

35: There, I've done it again

Have you ever opened your mouth to speak, and left a foot in there?
Have you ever worn something outlandish,
so your children pulled their hair?
Have you ever done something you shouldn't have done,
and driven your wife to despair?
Then I have to confess, I'm in the same mess, for I tell you – I've also been
there.

As a boy in short grey trousers, at my local Primary School
The teachers raised their eyes to heaven and dismissed me as a fool,
So I played the village idiot and acted rather cool,
Until one day I took it too far and almost drowned in a swimming pool.

I never really grew up, but suddenly found I was old,
Now looking back at mistakes I made leaves me somewhat cold.
I wish I'd lived the life I'd dreamed, the one where I was bold,
But my mouth kept running away from me, a problem I never solved.

I've a cupboard full of skeletons, they rattle in the dark,
I've dropped so many clangers, I fear I've left my mark,
Acting inappropriately and treating life as a bit of a lark,
I've stopped many a conversation with a clumsy and thoughtless remark.

I'd like to turn the clock back and try all over again,
Next time I'd do my utmost not to be such a boring old pain,
But truth be told I fear it's too late, besides, there's nothing to gain
So I'll live up to expectations – and continue just the same.

36: The moon's a balloon

The moon's a balloon, or so they say,
and the sun's a big sticky bun,
while the stars that shine are the sparkles from wine
sprayed up there when day is done.

That's nonsense I know, but suppose it was so,
and not just a figment of dreams,
then the clouds that float by in a bright summer sky
could be Mr Whippy ice creams.

Supposing the moon really is a balloon,
Neil Armstrong would make it go 'pop'
but the sticky old sun would still be a bun
with a glacé cherry on top.

As for the stars that sparkle at night,
splashed there from the best champagne,
I guess the excess – if there is, more or less
will eventually fall back as rain.

Okay, my imagination
is running away with me now.
My wife is once more bewildered
and wonders where and how
did this handsome hunk she married
lose the biggest part of his brain,
as well as the fortune he promised her?
Did that also go down the drain?

'Now who are you saying is crazy?'
I question the love of my life,
'Did I ever promise a fortune
when I asked you to be my wife?
All I said, my love, was before we're dead
we'll have a lot of fun.
So let's reach up and take a bite
from that bright red sticky bun.'

37: A song at dawn

There's a robin on a thorn bush, his breast an orange-red,
He woke up feeling perky while I was still in bed,
He made himself quite comfy, then raised his pretty head
To greet the morning with his song, and this is what he said:
Wake up my fellow songbirds, the dawn is on its way
There's never been one like it, this is a brand new day.
In homes all round the country folk in ignorance delay
Rising up to hear us sing – for this is what they say:

Is that the time? I'm weary still, another hour I need,
I can wait a bit for breakfast, I'm not ready yet to feed
And the birds out in the garden can hang on for their seed
So I'll close my eyes another hour to dream of my misdeeds.

You'd think they'd know much better, said the blackbird with a frown,
But when you think about it, would you live in a town?
With that he shook his feathers, before he settled down
To lead the songbird chorus in which he wore the crown.
The song thrush woke up with a start, as did the tiny wren,
A pigeon cooed, a magpie laughed, a jay cried out Amen
As one by one they checked the sun was on its way, and then
Began their rich dawn chorus unheard by any men.

But if you leave your bed before the alarm begins to ring
Then wander through a woodland early in the spring,
Your eyes will water freely when you hear the songbirds sing
And you'll know without a doubt that you're as rich as any king.

38: Lost – again

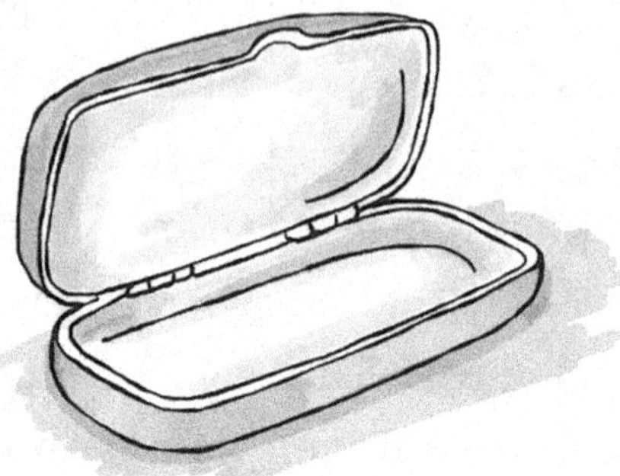

That's it! I'm done!
I can think of nothing more.
I've turned the place right upside down,
both in and out of doors.
I've searched throughout the kitchen,
I've been through all the drawers,
I've been down on my hands and knees
examining the floors.
I cannot think where next to look,
the cupboards have been done,
I've poked inside the kitchen waste
and that was not much fun.
I've shaken all the curtains
and looked beneath the chairs,
and all I found's a comb I'd lost
clogged with all my hairs.
But what about the cushions
on that sofa over there?
I tore each one wide open,
there's no feather left to spare.
I'm sure I had them breakfast time,

or was it late last night?
I know I had them with me
when I last turned off the light.
Now where would I have put them?
Where did I lay them down?
Don't say my wife has picked them up
and taken them to town.
She must be coming home right now
I'll meet her at the door
and ask if she remembers
where I put them once before.
Ah, here comes my beloved
I'll ask her right away.
Have you seen my brand new specs?
And then I hear her say:
you really are the limit;
a fool - but what the heck?
The glasses you've been looking for
are hanging round your neck.

39: Words of wisdom

When I was young and handsome (okay, when I was young),
Words of worldly wisdom dripped from my mother's tongue.
She'd sit me down beside her in her cosy wing-backed chair
And as she spoke her fingers twisted tangles in my hair.
Her voice was soft and gentle, you'd never hear her shout
So I listened to the things she'd say and never had a doubt.

'Yesterday's a dead one, Dear, tomorrow's yet to come,
All we have's this moment, so live it well my son.'

I've often thought about this and discovered it is true
So tried to pass it on to lots of others that I knew.
The past has had its day, there's no more that you can do
And tomorrow's just a dream for now, a distant unseen view.
But today – ah yes, - today is Now and now is all we've got
So gather every moment, use them well, don't watch the clock.

'Never look a gift horse in the mouth,' my old mum used to say
Then gave a little chuckle that sounded like a neigh!

Well, sad to say I've yet to have a horse bring me a gift,
Though once when injured in the hills, one did give me a lift.
I sat up on the saddle and there looked all around
Until the saddle slipped, and I tumbled to the ground.
But maybe that's the gift horse my mother spoke about,
So perhaps it's just as well I never looked inside its mouth.

'Don't count your chickens 'til they hatch,' were more wise words from Mum,
'For disappointment's all you'll get – remember that, my son.'

We had some chickens once, when I was just a lad
At the bottom of the garden with a coop made by my dad.
But there the broody mums-to-be sat tight upon their eggs,
Squatting there I wondered - were they born without two legs?
And then one morning early I heard a dreadful din
And discovered that a hungry fox had managed to get in.

'If you wake up grumpy,' one time my mother said,
'Make sure you don't get out the wrong side of your bed.'

Oh mother dear, I've often thought that really does sound trite
But had reason to reflect on that just the other night.
I woke up in the darkness, in a hurry for the loo,
My stomach churning wildly so I knew what I must do.
I pulled the duvet back and then leaped out of bed
Right into the bedroom wall on which I crashed my head.

I have a list of other words of wisdom from my mum
To keep me on the straight and narrow, and still have time for fun.
'A stitch in time saves nine,' she'd say – you should see how I can darn!
And 'where there's life there's hope' has helped me overcome all harm.
I'd like to think I've passed on all the wisdom that she shared
And the heart of hers that proved to all just how much she cared.

40: Ambition achieved

The world stretched far as I could see
when I was a boy at school.
No garden fence could keep me in
and my parents had no rule.
They did their best to encourage me
to wander and explore,
knowing the more that I could see
would help me see some more.

Fields and woodlands, hedgerow trees,
streams I'd crawl through on my knees,
broken branches, moss-green logs
ponds with tadpoles, ponds with frogs,
birds that nested high above,
all God's creatures drew my love.
All of this in my domain
where I'd wander time and again.

One day I saw a herd of deer
grazing in a park,
and then a lonesome badger
waddling in the dark.
I watched a single heron
standing all alone,
no breeze would move its feathers
like a statue made of stone.

The only building in my view,
a windmill perched upon a hill.
It stood two easy miles away,
in fact it stands there still.
When the wind blew on an autumn day
its sails would slowly turn
and the creaking of its timbers
is a sound for which I'd yearn.

Education passed me by,
my head was full of dreams,
instead of history lessons
I'd be busy building schemes,
ways to dodge convention
when the time was right
Imagination was my friend
throughout the day and night.

I left that school a simple lad
no certificates to my name.
I was just another failure
with myself alone to blame.

But oh what joy that brought me,
with my very own path to tread.
While my schoolmates made their fortunes
I lived my dreams instead.

Oh boy, how I have loved my life,
yet it's gone by much too fast.
And I wonder where I'd be right now
were I first and not the last.
Perhaps I'd be a millionaire,
with a butler near at hand,
living a life of luxury
in a mansion with lots of land.

Instead you'll find me in a field.
You'll know me by my hat.
I'll be gazing in the distance
and quite content at that.
In all these years of living
my eyes are still aglow
for I've achieved my old ambition
to be the UK's best scarecrow.